A Friendship
Problem

Mermicorns

Sparkle Magic
A Friendship Problem
The Invisible Mix-Up

Purrmaids

The Scaredy Cat
The Catfish Club
Seasick Sea Horse
Search for the Mermicorn
A Star Purr-formance
Quest for Clean Water
Kittens in the Kitchen
Merry Fish-mas
Kitten Campout

MERMICORNs 2

A Friendship Problem

by Sudipta Bardhan-Quallen

illustrations by Vivien Wu

A STEPPING STONE BOOK™
Random House 🏠 New York

Text copyright © 2021 by Sudipta Bardhan-Quallen
Cover art copyright © 2021 by Andrew Farley
Interior illustrations copyright © 2021 by Vivien Wu

Visit us on the Web!
rhcbooks.com

Educators and librarians, for a variety of teaching tools, visit us at
RHTeachersLibrarians.com

Library of Congress Cataloging-in-Publication Data
Names: Bardhan-Quallen, Sudipta, author. | Wu, Vivien, illustrator.
Title: A friendship problem / by Sudipta Bardhan-Quallen;
illustrated by Vivien Wu.
Description: First edition. | New York: Random House, [2021] | Series: Mermicorns; 2 | "A Stepping Stone book." | Audience: Ages 6–9. | Summary: "Mermicorns Sirena and Lily are excited to learn magic that helps express their true feelings, but when Sirena wants to invite old friends to their secret clubhouse, Lily becomes jealous. Can Sirena have old friends and new friends?"—Provided by publisher.
Identifiers: LCCN 2020031782 (print) | LCCN 2020031783 (ebook) |
ISBN 978-0-593-30876-9 (trade) | ISBN 978-0-593-30877-6 (lib. bdg.) |
ISBN 978-0-593-30878-3 (ebook)
Subjects: CYAC: Friendship—Fiction. | Emotions—Fiction. | Magic—Fiction. |
Mermaids—Fiction. | Unicorns—Fiction. | Cats—Fiction.
Classification: LCC PZ7.B25007 Fr 2021 (print) | LCC PZ7.B25007 (ebook) |
DDC [Fic]—dc23

Printed in the United States of America
10 9 8 7 6 5 4 3 2 1
First Edition

This book has been officially leveled by using
the F&P Text Level Gradient™ Leveling System.

To Lola,
with the awesome hair

1

The sun was about to rise. Everywhere in Seadragon Bay was peaceful and quiet.

Everywhere, except Lily's bedroom.

It was too early to be up. That's why Lily's big sister, Lotus, was sleeping. But that meant Lily couldn't sleep—because Lotus was snoring.

HONK-SHOO! HONK-SHOOOO!

Lily put in her earbuds. She turned on her new favorite song. Neighlor Swift's

voice began to sing "Wildest Streams."
But Lily could barely hear it over the snoring. She covered her head with her pillow
and turned up the volume. That didn't
help, either! Lotus was way too loud.

I can't sleep anymore, Lily thought.
She carefully slid out of bed. She got
dressed for school. Then she slipped out
of the bedroom.

Lily tried to stay very quiet as she
swam past her parents' room. Mom was
sleeping inside. She stopped for a moment
at the next door. That used to be her bedroom. But when her baby sister, Lynn, was
born, Lily moved in with Lotus. Now her
old room was Lynn's nursery.

Lily opened the nursery door a tiny bit.
Lynn was sleeping peacefully in her crib.
Her sister was so adorable! Even though
Lynn was the reason Lily had to share a

room with Lotus, Lily couldn't help but smile.

Softly, Lily closed the door again. *I guess I'll go eat breakfast,* she thought. But when she got to the kitchen, she gasped. Someone was there, making scrambled tuna eggs.

"Dad!" Lily exclaimed. "You're home early!"

"Shhhh," Dad whispered. "You'll wake your mother."

Most parents in Seadragon Bay worked during the day. But the hospital in town needed a doctor there all the time. Dr. Farrier was the doctor on call at night. That meant he left for work after Lily's family finished dinner. He usually got home around the time they sat down for breakfast. Today, though, Dad was home before Mom was even awake.

"The hospital wasn't busy last night," Dad neighed. "So I got to leave a little early. I thought I'd surprise my favorite girls with breakfast. But why are you up?"

Lily frowned. "Lotus is snoring again. I couldn't sleep through it. No one could!"

Dad smiled. "That's too bad. But since you're here, maybe you'll be my special helper?"

That turned Lily's frown into a great big grin. "I'd love to!" she replied.

During the week, Dad slept while Lily and Lotus were at school. He usually didn't wake up until right before dinner. That meant it was really hard for Lily to get time alone with him. *I guess I'm lucky that Lotus sounds like a hippo with a stuffy nose!*

Dad pointed to a bowl of mangoes. "Can you peel those for us to share, Lily?"

Lily floated over to the fruit. She and Dad worked side by side. She put three mango slices on each plate. He added a helping of scrambled tuna eggs.

"Do you think your mother and sister will want kelp waffles?" Dad asked.

Lily was just about to answer. But someone else did instead. "I want waffles!"

Lily spun around. "Lotus!" she exclaimed. "Why aren't you asleep?"

"I heard noises," Lotus replied.

Lily snorted. "You heard noises over the sound of your snoring?"

"I do *not* snore!" Lotus snapped. "Are you guys making breakfast? Can I help? I can make kelp waffles!"

"That would be great," Dad said.

Lily's jaw dropped. "But, Dad," she whined, "this was supposed to be *my* special time with you!"

"It's still special," Dad said. "Having Lotus here doesn't change that."

Lily spun around so Dad wouldn't see her frowning. *Yes, it does,* she thought. She didn't want to share him with her sister. But there was nothing she could do.

The three mermicorns finished making breakfast. The plates looked perfect to Lily. But Dad said, "I think there's something missing."

There were waffles, mangoes, and scrambled tuna eggs on every plate. "I don't see anything wrong," Lily said. "What's missing?"

"This," Dad said. As the girls watched, his horn started twinkling. A cloud of glitter floated toward the plates. There was a bright flash of light. "Now look," he said. His magic had added the word *Surprise* to each waffle.

"This is so much better, Dad," Lily agreed. She brought the plates to the table. Just as she finished, Mom floated into the kitchen carrying Lynn. She rubbed her eyes sleepily and almost swam right into Dad.

"Watch where you're swimming!" Dad said, laughing.

"You're home early!" Mom cried. She saw the food on the table. "What a nice surprise!"

"We know!" Lotus said. "Dad decorated the waffles!"

Mom looked delighted. Lynn was cooing happily. Everything tasted really good. Soon, Lily felt a little less grumpy. Having the whole family together was pretty nice.

"Are you hanging out with Sirena after school again?" Mom asked when it was time to leave for the Magic Academy.

Lily nodded. "I'll be home by dinner," she said.

"It's nice that the two of you have become such good friends," Dad said.

Lily agreed. She loved the time she spent with Sirena. Thinking of that made *all* her grumpiness disappear.

By the time she was on her way to Sirena's house, Lily couldn't wait to see her friend. *I'm going to make sure we do something super special today,* she thought. *Something only the two of us can do!*

2

The first time the girls met, Lily wasn't sure if she and Sirena were going to be friends. Even when they became partners in Ms. Trainor's class, things were a bit stormy. But then they got stuck in Barracuda Belt during a *real* storm. They helped each other and, like magic, their friendship began.

Sirena lived between Lily's house and the Magic Academy. That was one reason the girls decided to meet outside the Chevals' house before school in the morning. They could swim together the rest of the way.

The other reason to meet at Sirena's house was her oyster garden. On their first day at the Magic Academy, Sirena had given Lily a silver necklace. They agreed that every time they learned a new bit of mermicorn magic, they would add a pearl to their necklaces.

The first magical skill that Ms. Trainor taught the class was how to make their horns glow. It didn't seem very exciting at first. But it came in handy during that storm! Lily and Sirena had been practicing that magic every chance they got. They finally felt like they'd really learned it. Today was the day they would pick out their first pearls.

Lily swam up to the Chevals' house. Mrs. Cheval opened the door.

"Good morning, Mrs. Cheval," Lily said.

"Good morning, Lily," Mrs. Cheval replied. "Come on in. Sirena will be ready in a minute."

"I'm just finishing a sea mail," Sirena called from the other room.

"Are you ready for your first pearl,

Lily?" Mrs. Cheval asked. "Show me what you've learned."

Lily took a deep breath. She closed her eyes and found her sparkle. Then she said, "Pickle tree, manatee, let there be . . . light!" The twinkles soon became a bright glow. "I did it!" Lily exclaimed. "It was easy peasy, turtle squeezy!"

"That was great!" Mrs. Cheval neighed. "And as you get better at magic, you won't even have to say the magic words out loud."

"But they're so much fun to say!" Sirena said as she swam into the room.

"Are you finally ready, Sirena?" Lily

asked. She winked so her friend would know she was just squidding around.

Sirena nodded. "Let's go pick out our pearls!"

The mermicorns floated to the oyster garden. The girls were so excited that they picked the first oysters they saw. They carefully opened the shells.

"My pearl is blue!" Sirena said.

"And mine is yellow!" Lily added.

Mrs. Cheval helped the fillies put the pearls on their necklaces. "Beautiful," she said. "Now you'd better get to school. I want you each to earn your next pearl!"

Sirena kissed her mother's cheek. "Hey, Mom," she said, "is it still fine for us to go to that clubhouse I found?"

Mrs. Cheval nodded.

Lily raised her eyebrows. *What is Sirena talking about?*

"Hopefully," Sirena continued, "we can make it *purr-fect*. Get it?"

Mrs. Cheval and Sirena giggled. Lily smiled, even though she didn't understand what was so funny.

On the way to the Magic Academy, Lily asked, "Did you find a clubhouse?"

"Yes!" Sirena said. "But it's a surprise. You have to wait until after school."

"Really?" Lily groaned. She hated waiting!

"It'll be worth it!" Sirena said. "I *purr-omise*!"

Lily sighed. "If this surprise is important to you," she said, "I'll go along with it. That's what friends do."

Sirena grinned. "I knew I could count on you!"

3

Lily really didn't want to wait for Sirena's surprise. Luckily, once they were in Ms. Trainor's classroom, it was easy to think about something else. Ms. Trainor had a new lesson for the class. Lily knew she had to pay attention to learn it well.

"We've been talking about how your feelings affect mermicorn magic," Ms. Trainor began. "When you feel something positive, it can be easier to make something magical happen. But if you're like me, it's not always easy to understand what you are feeling."

Sirena raised her hoof. "How can we get better at understanding our feelings?"

"Talking about our feelings like we do in class is one way," Ms. Trainor replied. "But it's not always easy to find the right words for our feelings. Especially if we aren't sure how we feel."

"My family always knows how I'm feeling by the music I'm listening to," Lily said.

"Do you always listen to the same songs?" Ms. Trainor asked.

Lily shook her head. "There are some songs I play when I'm excited. There are others for when I'm upset." She grinned. "I have a special playlist for when my sister is talking about something boring, like mane styles!"

Everyone laughed.

"Music can certainly help you figure out your feelings," Ms. Trainor said. "I like to write in my diary about my feelings."

"So do I!" Sirena added. "Sometimes I don't know how to talk about how I feel. But it's easier to write the correct words down on paper."

"We need to understand our feelings to be good at mermicorn magic," Ms. Trainor continued. "But magic can also help us get better at understanding our feelings. Today, I'm going to teach you how to turn your feelings into a picture."

Lily glanced at Sirena. "What is she talking about?" she whispered. "You can't see feelings."

At the front of the classroom, Ms. Trainor held up a blank piece of paper. She found her sparkle. Then she said, "Orange peel, harbor seal, show me how I really feel!"

As the class watched, the piece of paper started to twinkle, just like Ms. Trainor's horn. When the twinkles disappeared, the paper wasn't blank anymore. It had little gold hearts sprinkled all over it.

The students oohed and aahed. "That's beautiful!" Aqua exclaimed.

"Thank you," Ms. Trainor replied. "Right now, I feel excited to be your teacher. I feel grateful for a job that I love. Those feelings are beautiful to me. So my magic made something that I think looks beautiful."

Misty asked, "Can I use this magic to decorate my whole room with pretty things?"

Ms. Trainor propped the paper up on her desk. Then she turned to the class. "That's a good question," she said. "You could use this magic to decorate. But there are two things you need to keep in mind. First, there are times when our feelings create something beautiful. But the purpose of this magic isn't to make the world beautiful. Sometimes your feelings won't be bright and colorful like mine are right now. This magic will help you be honest about your feelings."

"But if we do make something beautiful with this magic, how long will it last?" Lily asked. "Will it stay like that forever?"

Ms. Trainor smiled. "That's the second thing you need to know!" she neighed. "It would be nice if our positive feelings lasted forever. But that's not how it works. No feeling—positive or negative—lasts forever." She pointed to the paper on her desk. "Some feelings last a really long time. Some feelings pass quickly. This magic will last as long as your feelings last."

Lily leaned over toward Sirena. "I bet this magic would still be a good way to decorate something," she whispered.

Sirena nodded. "If we can learn the magic quickly," she said, "we could use it

to decorate the clubhouse! I really want to make it a special place for friendships!"

"Are you talking about the clubhouse you don't want to tell me about?" Lily teased.

Sirena winked. "I guess you still have to wait and see!"

4

Most of the students wanted to start practicing their new magic lesson right away. But Ms. Trainor had a different idea. "Let's have our snack and then a quick recess," she said.

The class groaned. But they stopped when Ms. Trainor showed them a tray of sea carrot cupcakes!

"I love those!" Toby exclaimed.

Ms. Trainor told the class to take their

snacks to the courtyard. She didn't need to say it twice! Everyone grabbed a cupcake and swam outside.

In the courtyard, Lily sat down on her favorite coral bench. Sirena sat next to her. They ate in silence. The cupcake was so good, Lily finished it in less than a minute! "I absolutely love sea carrot cake," she said.

"I can see that," Sirena joked. She plopped the last bite of her cupcake into her mouth.

"I guess you like it, too!" Lily said.

Sirena nodded.

"Too bad we don't have more cupcakes," Lily said. She looked out at the mermicorns in the courtyard. Some were playing Freeze Tag. Others were playing Simon Says. "Do you want to join one of the games, Sirena?"

Sirena shook her head. "I have a better idea," she neighed. "Let's practice the new magic!"

Lily grinned. "That *is* a better idea! What should we practice on?"

Sirena popped up. "How about this?" she said. She pointed to the seat of the bench.

"Another great idea!" Lily replied. She floated off the bench, too.

"Do you want to go first?" Sirena asked.

"I'd love to!" Lily said. She closed her eyes and found her sparkle right away. Then she said, "Orange peel, harbor seal, show me how I really feel!"

The seat of the bench started to twinkle, just like the paper had in Ms. Trainor's classroom. And then the seat was covered in pictures of cupcakes and hearts!

"I guess I know how you are feeling!" Sirena exclaimed. "This is great!"

"No," Lily cried. "This is terrible!"

Sirena frowned. "What do you mean? Did the magic show the wrong feeling?"

Lily shook her head. "No, I'm definitely feeling like I want more cupcakes."

"Then why is this terrible?" Sirena asked.

"I can't look at all those cupcakes

without getting hungry again!" Lily said, laughing.

Sirena rolled her eyes. "You are always joking, Lily."

Lily's smile disappeared. "I *never* joke about cupcakes," she said in a serious voice.

Both girls giggled.

"What's so funny?" a voice asked. Lily and Sirena spun around. It was Misty.

"Hi, Misty," Lily said. "We were just joking about cupcakes."

Misty floated closer to the bench. She saw the cupcake pictures. "Were you two practicing the magic Ms. Trainor just showed us?"

Sirena nodded.

"Can I practice, too?" Misty asked.

Lily was about to answer, but Sirena spoke first. "Sure, Misty," she said.

Lily's mouth snapped shut. *I was going to say no,* she thought. It wasn't that she didn't like Misty. It was just that she and Sirena always spent recess together. She didn't want to share her friend with anyone else.

"Oh, look," Sirena said. She pointed at the bench. "I guess Lily isn't hungry anymore."

The cupcake pictures were fading

before their eyes. Lily gulped. *It must be because my feelings changed,* she thought. At that moment, she was disappointed that she couldn't have time alone with Sirena. That feeling was stronger than how much she loved cupcakes.

Luckily, Sirena and Misty didn't notice. As soon as the cupcake pictures were completely gone, Sirena said, "I'm so excited for a turn to try."

"Me too!" Misty replied. "Do you want to go first, Sirena?"

"We can go together," Sirena said. "I'll take this side of the bench. You work on that one."

Misty floated to the far side of the bench. Sirena stayed where she was. Lily backed away to give them room.

The fillies found their sparkles and then said the magic words at the same time. A cloud of twinkles floated from each of their horns and settled over either side of the bench. It took a little longer for the twinkles to disappear than before. But when they did, Sirena's half of the bench was covered in pictures of rainbows.

Misty's half was covered in silver scallop shells.

Lily floated closer to get a better look. "You both felt excited," she neighed. "So why do the pictures look so different?"

Sirena and Misty shrugged.

Lily scratched her mane. "We have to talk to Ms. Trainor about this," she said.

"Good thing it's time to go back to class," Sirena said.

5

All the students swam back to class. Most went right to their seats. But Lily, Sirena, and Misty stopped at Ms. Trainor's desk.

"We have a question," Lily said. "We were practicing the new magic at recess. Sirena and Misty both felt excited. But the pictures that their magic created weren't the same."

Ms. Trainor smiled. "You three are getting ahead of my lesson! Go back to your desks. We'll talk about this with the whole class."

When all the mermicorns had settled, Ms. Trainor said, "I just got a question from some of you about our magic lesson. Two students decided to practice during recess. They both felt excited. But their magic made different pictures. Can anyone guess why that happened?"

The students looked at each other. Some shrugged. No one said anything.

Finally, Lily raised a hoof. "Could it be because we can feel different kinds of excited?"

"Exactly!" Ms. Trainor said, grinning. "Our feelings don't always feel the same. So there isn't just one picture that means excited or happy or disappointed. The picture this magic will create for you is just another hint about what you are feeling.

You will still have to figure out what the picture really means."

Some of the students nodded. But others still looked confused. So Ms. Trainor continued, "Here's another example. We all feel frustrated sometimes. But we aren't frustrated by the same things, right?"

"I'm frustrated when my parents make me clean my room," Toby said.

"I love cleaning my room!" Aqua neighed. "Putting everything where it belongs makes me feel calm."

"I get frustrated when my sister won't sleep," a student named Pearl said.

"Well, I get frustrated when my sister *does* sleep," Lily said. "My sister snores!"

That made the mermicorns laugh.

"As you can see, something that frustrates one mermicorn might be wonderful for another," Ms. Trainor said. "That's true of all our feelings." She passed out a blank paper to each of her students. "Let's do an activity that will make this really clear. I'll play a song for you. When it's done, I want you to try to do the new magic."

The teacher held up her shell phone. Music began to play. Lily recognized the song right away. "It's Neighlor Swift!"

she whispered to Sirena. "This is her new song!"

For a few minutes, the notes of "Wildest Streams" filled the classroom. At the end, Ms. Trainor said, "Go ahead, everyone. Let's see what your magic will create."

Neighlor Swift had put Lily in a great mood. She didn't even have to close her eyes to find her sparkle. She concentrated on the blank paper and said, "Orange peel, harbor seal, show me how I really feel!"

The other students did the same thing. All around, there were clouds of shimmers and twinkles. Lily's paper was left covered in bright pink and purple musical notes that matched her mane. "Oh, look!" she said. She held her paper out to Sirena.

"It looks like that song made you very happy," Sirena said. "The picture is bright and cheerful."

Lily glanced at Sirena's paper. Hers had musical notes on it, too. But those notes were simple and black. Lily frowned. "You don't like the song?" she asked.

Sirena shrugged. "It's fine. Listening to it is fun. I like Bruno Mares more, though."

Lily rolled her eyes. "Neighlor Swift is so much more talented than Bruno Mares." She grinned. "But I guess I'll still be your friend."

Sirena giggled. "That's very nice of you!"

Ms. Trainor told everyone to hold up their papers. Some of the students' pictures were as bright and colorful as Lily's. Those were also the students who were smiling like they really liked the song. Other pictures were more simple, like Sirena's. Toby's picture was different from the others. His paper was covered in gray clouds. Ms. Trainor floated over to him. "Can you tell us how the song made you feel, Toby?" she asked.

Toby shrugged. "I honestly do not understand why mermicorns like Neighlor Swift. None of her songs make any sense to me."

Most of the class laughed. But Lily gasped. "How can you even say that, Toby?" She couldn't believe there was anyone under the sea who didn't like Neighlor Swift at least a little bit!

Luckily for Toby, he didn't have to answer. Sirena shouted, "Look at your paper, Lily!"

Lily turned away from Toby. The pink

and purple music notes were fading away as she watched. Soon, her paper was blank again.

Lily realized what was happening. "It's because my feelings changed," she said. "I felt happy and excited when Ms. Trainor played the song. But when Toby said what he said, I felt shocked."

"Ms. Trainor told us the magic only lasts as long as the feeling lasts," Sirena said. "Look!" She held up her paper. "Right now, I feel curious about the magic. That's different from what I felt after the song." The music notes on Sirena's paper had faded as well.

"Let's try again!" Lily exclaimed.

6

Ms. Trainor's students spent the rest of the afternoon practicing the lesson. It was interesting to see the different pictures that the magic created. It was also interesting that the magic looked different even when the mermicorns felt the same feelings.

When Ms. Trainor played "Upstream Funk," Sirena seemed just as excited as Lily had been after "Wildest Streams." But the picture her magic created wasn't of colorful music notes. Her paper was covered in rainbow-colored sunglasses. They looked just like the ones that Bruno Mares wore in the music video.

By the time the bell rang at the end of the school day, Lily and Sirena didn't need much more practice with the new lesson. "Do you know what that means?" Sirena asked.

Lily shook her head.

"It means we don't have homework!" Sirena squealed. "And we can go to the clubhouse!"

"I forgot all about the clubhouse!" Lily exclaimed.

Lily and Sirena swam through the streets of the town. When they reached the town gates, Lily asked, "Why are we leaving Seadragon Bay?"

"It's in Barracuda Belt," Sirena said.

Lily frowned. "That means it's not in town," she said.

"But it's also not *not* in town," Sirena replied. "We'll still be inside the rock walls. That's why my parents said it was fine for us to go to the clubhouse alone." She touched Lily's shoulder. "Don't worry. We'll be safe."

The girls crossed Barracuda Belt and reached the rock walls. Sirena pointed to a giant elkhorn coral in the distance.

BARRACUDA BELT!

"The entrance is hidden behind that. You can't even see it unless you swim right up to it."

They floated to a small gap in the rocks. "Are you sure about this?" Lily asked. She peeked into the gap. "It looks really dark in there."

"Good thing we know what to do about that!" Sirena's horn began to twinkle, and she said, "Pickle tree, manatee, let there be . . . light!"

Sirena's magic lit up most of the dark rocky tunnel. Now Lily could see that it was just big enough for the two of them to swim through. Sirena's light didn't quite reach the end of the tunnel. But it was clearly brighter there. "Is that where we're going?" Lily asked.

Sirena nodded. "Come on!"

Lily knew that Sirena was very excited

about the clubhouse. But when they reached the end of the tunnel, Lily's mouth dropped open. It was more amazing than she had imagined! The underwater cave had a rock floor and rock walls. The floor was smooth and shiny. In the center, there was a table coral with a large flat top. It would be perfect for sharing snacks, doing art projects, or reading books. There was even a family of clown fish who lived under the table coral. They were like a colorful decoration. Red corals grew in branches on the rock walls all the way up to the surface of the water. They gave the cave a warm glow.

The top of the cave was open, so sunlight filtered in. That kept the cave from being dark. The girls swam up and poked their heads out of the water. The walls reached high into the sky. There were ledges in the rock walls above the surface of the ocean to sit on. The girls could enjoy some sunshine without worrying about being seen by humans!

"Isn't this a great place for practicing magic?" Sirena asked. She twirled in the water.

Lily nodded. "I love it. Thank you for bringing me here."

Sirena pulled Lily into a hug. "I told you I wanted to make this a special place for friends."

Lily was just about to say how nice it was that Sirena found something for just the two of them. But Sirena interrupted her.

"We need to hurry," Sirena said. "I want everything to be perfect before Angel, Coral, and Shelly get here."

Lily gasped. The clubhouse wasn't for her and Sirena to share. Sirena had wanted to make it special for *other* friends the whole time!

7

"Who are Angel, Coral, and Shelly?" Lily asked softly.

"They're my friends!" Sirena replied. "I haven't seen them in a while. So I invited them to come meet me here this afternoon. That's the sea mail I was writing this morning!"

Lily glanced at Sirena out of the corner of her eye. "Are Coral, Shelly, and Angel friends from your old school?"

"From school?" Sirena said. "No, I met them somewhere else. I was out exploring the ocean one day. I got a little lost—but then I ended up finding them!" She grinned. "They live in a different town. But it's not too far away, so they should be here soon. I think they will love this place!"

Lily looked away so Sirena wouldn't see her frowning. *Sirena is* my *best friend,* she thought. *I don't want to share her with these other mermicorns!*

"Today's magic lesson gave me an idea," Sirena continued. She poked out of the water near the back wall of the cave. "Come here and I'll tell you about it," Sirena called.

If I don't go along with her plans, she'll know I don't want to meet her friends,

Lily thought. There was no way she could say no to Sirena. She sighed.

Even though Lily wasn't far from Sirena, it felt like it took forever to reach her friend. All her excitement about the clubhouse had disappeared. It didn't feel so special to have to share the clubhouse—and to have to share her best friend.

Sirena didn't notice, though. She was positively bubbly about her plans for the clubhouse. "I thought you could decorate that side of the wall with magic," Sirena said, pointing. "I'll decorate this one. It'll be super special!"

Lily frowned. "I don't even know these friends," she said. "Maybe you should just do it." She noticed some bits of kelp floating around. "I'll clean all this up."

Sirena rolled her eyes. "Lily!" she exclaimed. "We're in the ocean. You can't clean all the kelp out of the ocean." She grabbed Lily's hoof and pulled her closer to the back wall. "Think of this as practicing our lesson," she said. She pointed. "Go ahead."

Lily was fairly certain that jealousy and frustration would not make a pretty picture. *I can't let Sirena know how I feel,* she thought. *What am I going to do?*

Lily decided it would be best not to do

anything. *I can't do this magic. Not in front of Sirena.* So she closed her eyes. She found her sparkle. But then she said the *wrong* words on purpose. "Oar and wheel, charmer seal, show me how I really feel!"

Nothing happened.

Sirena floated over and patted Lily's shoulder. "I think you forgot the words," she said. "You're supposed to say 'orange peel, harbor seal,' not 'oar and wheel, charmer seal.'"

"Oh, you're right," Lily replied. "You're better at this magic than I am. Maybe you should decorate everything." It didn't feel good to lie to Sirena. *But I can't tell her the truth*, she thought.

Unfortunately, Sirena shook her head. "I'm not going to let you give up!" she exclaimed. "That's not what a friend would do. You have to try again!"

Lily couldn't believe it! Now she was feeling jealous, frustrated, *and* guilty for hiding things from her friend. *I don't need a picture to tell me how I really feel,* she thought. *I need time to find something positive to think about.*

Suddenly, Lily had an idea. "You go first, Sirena," she neighed. "I need to watch someone get it right." *When Sirena does a perfect job with the magic, I'll be proud of her,* she thought. She smiled. Feeling proud would help her create something beautiful on her side of the wall.

"If you say so," Sirena replied. She turned toward the wall and closed her eyes. She found her sparkle. Then she said, "Orange peel, harbor seal, show me how I really feel!"

Just like at school, the magic made twinkles appear. But the wall was much bigger than the paper. The twinkling only started in one corner of the wall. Lily could tell Sirena was really concentrating. Slowly, the twinkles spread.

"Keep trying, Sirena," Lily whispered. "It's working!"

Soon, the twinkles covered the entire side of the wall. Sirena opened her eyes. Lily floated next to her and put an arm around her shoulders. Then the girls watched the wall together. It seemed to glitter for a minute longer. Then, all of a sudden, the twinkles were gone. The picture that Sirena's magic had created was amazing. There was a rainbow background with hearts everywhere. But the

hearts weren't all the same. In fact, Lily saw three different designs. Some were black and white. Some were orange with stripes. And some were pure white.

Lily didn't know what the different colors meant. But they were bright and cheery. Even without a picture, Lily could tell that Sirena couldn't wait for her friends to arrive.

8

"Your turn, Lily," Sirena said.

Lily gulped. She was truly proud of how well Sirena could use the magic they learned today. But it still hurt that Sirena didn't want to just spend time with her. Especially since Lily didn't want to share her friend with anyone else.

Lily tried to push those thoughts away. She closed her eyes. She did her best to concentrate on being proud of Sirena.

That helped her find her sparkle. She said the magic words. She opened one eye a little bit to see what was happening.

Glitter began to spread across the wall. Lily felt butterfly fish fluttering in her tummy. *I hope this works!*

But when the wall stopped twinkling, Lily knew she'd made a mistake. Thinking about being proud of Sirena couldn't hide what she was really feeling. Her side of the wall was covered in dark storm clouds. Drops of rain fell from the clouds. Everything was dark and gray.

Lily gulped again. She thought, *How am I going to explain this to Sirena?*

Sirena floated closer to Lily's side of the wall. She was looking at the picture very closely.

"I don't know what happened," Lily

tried to explain. "I must have done something wrong."

But it didn't look like Sirena believed that. She frowned. "Ms. Trainor said this magic shows you how you really feel, even when you can't find the right words for it." She pointed to the wall. "Dark blue storm clouds. That looks like you are upset." She turned to face Lily. "Are you pretending that you want to be here? That you want to meet my friends?"

Lily stared down at the ocean floor. "It isn't that I don't want to meet your friends," she said. "I just really like spending time just you and me."

"So you've been lying to me?" Sirena asked.

Lily nodded sadly. "I'm really sorry," she said.

Sirena didn't respond. Lily could tell she wasn't feeling happy and excited anymore. It was clear from her face. It was also clear from the way the magic on the wall was fading away.

"I think I should leave," Lily said. "You can still get the clubhouse ready for your friends."

Sirena crossed her arms. "I think that's a good idea."

Lily turned away. She didn't want Sirena to see that she was about to cry. She hurried toward the tunnel. She didn't use her magic for light in the tunnel this time. She just swam through in the dark. *I ruined everything,* she thought. *I lied to Sirena. She probably doesn't even want to be friends anymore.* She didn't know how to fix things with Sirena. She just wanted to get out of there as quickly as she could.

Lily darted out of the tunnel. Then she sat on the ocean floor behind the giant elkhorn coral. She finally let the tears fall.

Suddenly, Lily heard voices. "I think this is the place," one voice said.

"Are you sure?" asked another voice.

"Can I see the note?" asked a third voice.

Those must be Sirena's friends, Lily thought. The last thing she wanted to do was meet them. She peeked carefully out from behind the elkhorn to see where they were coming from.

But it wasn't Sirena's friends! Those voices weren't coming from mermicorns! The three creatures she saw were half-kitten and half-mermaid. One had silky white fur. Another had orange fur with stripes. The last one had black-and-white fur. They looked like creatures called purrmaids that Lily had read about. *But they can't be purrmaids!* she thought. Purrmaids weren't real! At least, that's what her parents had always told her. But there were definitely three kitten mermaids floating right there in front of her!

The purrmaids gathered around their map. Lily couldn't hear what they were saying. But it didn't matter. There shouldn't be purrmaids in Barracuda

Belt. The warning signs should have kept them out! *If they aren't scared of barracudas,* Lily thought, *they must be scary themselves!*

Now Lily really didn't know what to do. She could swim back into the clubhouse and be safe. But Sirena didn't want her there. *And what if the purrmaids follow me into the clubhouse?*

Lily could do something to get the purrmaids' attention. Then she could lure them away from the clubhouse entrance. That way, Sirena would be safe. She shivered. That was a scary thought. But it was what a good friend would do.

Lily took a deep breath. She gathered her courage. Then she popped out from behind the elkhorn coral. But she wasn't able to say anything to make the purrmaids notice her. They'd already found her!

"Excuse me," the orange purrmaid said. "Do you know a mermicorn named Sirena?"

Lily tried to answer, but nothing came out! She just opened and closed her mouth a few times. She must have looked like a fish!

The black-and-white purrmaid leaned toward her friends. She purred, "I don't know if she understands us."

"That's weird," the white one replied. "Sirena always understands us."

"You know Sirena?" Lily asked. The

purrmaids nodded. "Are you the friends she invited?"

"Yes, we are," said the orange purrmaid. "I'm Coral." She pointed to her friends. "This is Shelly, and this is Angel."

All of a sudden, Lily realized why the hearts in Sirena's picture looked the way they did. They matched the purrmaids' fur!

"Sirena said to meet her at a clubhouse she found," Angel said. "But we're having trouble finding it."

"Are you Lily?" Shelly asked.

Lily frowned. "How did you know that?"

"Sirena told us all about you!" Coral said.

"She made you sound so cool, we couldn't wait to meet you!" Angel added.

9

At first, what the purrmaids said made Lily feet great. But then she thought about how she'd hurt Sirena's feelings. *Sirena wanted her friends to meet me,* she thought. *I'm the one who didn't want to meet them. I wish I hadn't been so selfish.*

"Did you hear me, Lily?" Angel asked.

"I'm sorry," Lily said to Angel. "I wasn't paying attention. What did you ask?"

"Do you know where Sirena is?" Shelly said.

Lily nodded. "I can show you. But I need to know something first."

"What?" Coral asked.

"Purrmaids are definitely not dangerous, right?" Lily asked.

Shelly rolled her eyes. "Why do mermicorns always think purrmaids are scary?"

Lily said, "It must be the claws!" Then she realized that Angel had made the same joke—at the same time! The two girls looked at each other and giggled.

"Sirena never told me you had my sense of humor," Angel said. "I would have asked to meet you earlier!"

"Before we go," Coral said, "I have a question." She bit her lip and looked away. "Are there really barracudas here in this reef?"

"Coral can be a little bit of a scaredy cat," Angel teased.

"A barracuda bite can really hurt!" Coral exclaimed.

"I agree," Lily said. "I'm scared of barracudas, too. I think it's smart to stay away from anything that might bite me!"

Coral smiled. "Thank you for being on my side," she whispered to Lily.

"No problem!" Lily replied. "If there were really barracudas in Barracuda Belt, I would never swim here! I don't think you're a scaredy cat. I think you're a smarty cat!"

Lily was about to tell the purrmaids to follow her when someone spoke. "What's going on here?"

Lily spun around. It was Sirena!

The purrmaids pulled Sirena into a group hug. "It's so great to see you!" Angel exclaimed.

"Thank you for inviting us," Coral added.

"We've met your friend Lily," Shelly purred. She waved for Lily to come closer.

Lily swam up to face Sirena. "I was just showing your friends how to get into the clubhouse," she said. She lowered her eyes. "Before I go home."

"Don't go home, Lily," Sirena said, floating closer. She touched Lily's shoulder. "I want you to stay."

Lily raised her eyes. "You do?"

Now Sirena hugged Lily.

"Thank you," Lily whispered. "I really am sorry for hiding my feelings from you before. I was just so jealous. Sometimes I get that way. I don't always like sharing the mermicorns I love."

"Oh, Lily," Sirena neighed. "I get that way, too. But I don't want them to be *my* friends. I hope they'll become *our* friends."

"I hope that, too," Lily replied. "And I need to remember that we don't have to be alone for our time to be special."

The girls smiled at each other. Then Lily asked, "Were you coming out to find me?"

Sirena nodded. "Your picture began to fade. So I knew something about your feelings had changed." She winked. "And I missed you, too. I didn't want to keep fighting."

"But wait," Lily said. "Does that mean there are no decorations left in the clubhouse?"

"The walls are blank again," Sirena said.

Suddenly, Lily had an idea. "Give the purrmaids a short tour of Barracuda Belt," she said. "I need a few minutes."

"What are you going to do?" Sirena asked.

"I'm going to make sure the clubhouse is a special place for friends," Lily answered.

10

As Sirena led Coral, Angel, and Shelly through Barracuda Belt, Lily raced to the clubhouse. She swam right up to the ocean's surface and faced the back wall. This time felt very different from the last time. She wasn't feeling jealous or disappointed. She wasn't trying to hide anything. This time, Lily felt grateful that Sirena wasn't still angry. She felt happy that the purrmaids already thought she was cool. She felt eager to get to know the purrmaids herself. But mostly, Lily felt excited about making new friends.

Lily's horn was already sparkling. She closed her eyes and said, "Orange peel, harbor seal, show me how I really feel!"

Lily took a few deep breaths before she opened her eyes. The wall wasn't glittering anymore. It had a very simple picture on it. There were no traces of storm clouds. Instead, there were five stars arranged in a circle. Each star had different colors— black and white, orange, white, rainbow, and pink and purple. There were gold lines connecting each star to all the rest. The lines made another star that shone brightly on the wall.

Lily smiled. She heard the other girls swimming through the tunnel. They would be in the clubhouse any minute.

I finished just in time, she thought. She sat on one of the rock ledges and waited for everyone to reach her.

Sirena gave Angel, Shelly, and Coral a quick tour of the underwater part of the clubhouse. They oohed and aahed at all the cool parts. Then Sirena led the purrmaids up to Lily.

"What did you think?" Lily asked them.

But none of the purrmaids said anything. They were all looking at the rock wall. Their mouths were open, and they looked amazed.

Finally, Angel said, "It's beautiful."

"Lily did all of this," Sirena said.

"It's paw-some," Shelly purred.

The girls swam down to the table coral. Shelly had brought some snacks to share. "I hope you like sushi, Lily," she said.

"Of course I do!" Lily replied.

The five friends passed Shelly's sushi rolls around. Then Sirena had an idea. "We should come up with a name for our group," she said. "How about the Sisterhood of the Secret Hideout?"

"Oooh!" Angel exclaimed. "I like that!"

"And it would be great if we were really all sisters!" Coral added.

Shelly snorted. "You guys only think sisters are great because you don't have any. Trust me, my big sisters can be a real pain in the tail!"

Lily nodded. "She's right! My sister actually keeps me up at night." She winked. "She snores really loudly!"

"I think you and I are the only ones who truly understand, Lily," Shelly said, smiling.

"I don't think we need to be sisters," Lily said. "I think it will be nice to be really good friends."

"Maybe even *purr-fect* friends!" Sirena joked.

Everyone laughed. They finished their snacks and swam back up to the rock ledges. The purrmaids wanted to look at the decorated wall again.

Lily realized that the wall was glowing

even more brightly than it was before. The colors were richer. The gold lines between the stars were more shimmery. *It must be because I'm more excited about these new friends than I was when I did the magic,* she thought. She had learned that she had something in common with each of the purrmaids. She couldn't wait to joke around with Angel some more. She loved that Shelly understood how tough it could be to have sisters! And she was glad that she and Coral could team up on doing the smart thing even when their other friends wanted to break some rules. Lily's feelings about the purrmaids were stronger, so the picture actually looked more dazzling!

The purrmaids admired the wall again. "You put so much work into

decorating this clubhouse!" Coral said. "It's magical!"

Lily winked at Sirena. "I guess it is!" she said. "But it won't always look like this."

The purrmaids looked confused. "But why would you change it?" Angel asked.

"Every time we all meet up here," Lily said, "Sirena and I will make sure the clubhouse is decorated."

"It'll match how we feel," Sirena added. "That way it will be special each time."

"You two are fin-tastic," Shelly said. "We are lucky to have friends like you."

Lily grinned. "I think we're all lucky to have each other. I can't wait to see what kind of fun we'll have together!"

Lily and Sirena are so excited to learn
how to make things disappear.
It's a tricky kind of magic . . .
but what could possibly go wrong?

Read on for a sneak peek.

The books on the lower level of the library were organized by type of magic. Each shelf had a sign. Sirena and Lily swam around until they saw the one that said INVISIBILITY.

There were many shelves of books in the section. "I don't know where to start," Lily said. "Maybe this one? Or this one?"

Sirena shrugged. "Just pick one that looks cool." She didn't bother to read all the book titles. She just grabbed the one that had the fanciest spine. "*The*

Disappearing Art of Invisibility," she read. *"Discover Forgotten Magic."* She turned the cover so Lily could see. "This sounds interesting!"

The girls sat down and began flipping through the pages. "There are fourteen different types of invisibility magic," Sirena said.

"I didn't know that," Lily replied.

"I wonder why we need so many," Sirena said.

"It's probably in the book," Lily said.

Sirena flipped to the next page. "It says here that 'all invisibility magic makes the target invisible.' That doesn't explain why there are so many types."

Lily snorted. "There's still a lot of book left! You haven't finished reading it." She got up from the table. "Before we find that answer, we need to work on our project." She went back to the shelf. After looking for a long time, she took out another two books. They were two parts of *Invisibility Through Mermicorn History.* "These might be more useful."

Sirena frowned. She didn't want to learn how *other* mermicorns used magic. She wanted to learn how to *do* magic! But Lily was right. They needed to finish the assignment. She closed her book and pushed it away. Lily put one of the history books in front of Sirena. She sat down and opened the other one.

The fillies read quietly for a while. Then Lily giggled. "I just read about a mermicorn student who accidentally made his final exam invisible. He had to do the entire year of school over again!"

"I bet he learned how to use invisibility magic the right way after that!" Sirena replied.

"Actually," Lily neighed, "he never used invisibility magic again!"

"I found something, too," Sirena said. She slid the book closer to Lily. "It's about Tiger Shark Trench and why it's so dangerous."

Tiger Shark Trench was a place where mermicorns were never supposed to go. Tiger sharks lived there, which is how it got its name. There were also other scary sharks like hammerheads and blue sharks. But the most dangerous animal who lived in Tiger Shark Trench was supposedly a giant great white shark. No one had seen the great white in many years—but then again, no one really went to Tiger Shark Trench.

"It says here that many, many years ago, a mermicorn was swimming alone in Tiger Shark Trench. He swam into a great white shark, and he tried to make himself invisible to hide. Except he made the shark invisible instead! So now the shark can hunt without ever being seen."

"So did he get eaten by the shark?" Lily asked.

"It doesn't say," Sirena said. "But probably. I mean, how do you get away from an invisible shark?"

"But if he was eaten," Lily said, "who told all the rest of the mermicorns about the invisible shark?"

"That's a good point," Sirena said. "Do you think some of the stories about magical mistakes are made up? Like, they make us learn them so we are sure to be careful using magic?"

Lily shrugged. "I don't know. I don't think Ms. Trainor would try to fool us."

"But what if she was fooled by the same stories when she was a foal?" Sirena asked. "Maybe magic doesn't make as many problems as grown-ups say it does. Maybe they just tell us that so we don't try magic without them." Her eyes grew wide. "Do you know what that means?"

Lily shook her head.

Sirena laughed. "That means we *can* try new magic today!"